Nix Alba:

Vita in Morte

Lanie Goodell

Printed in the United States of America

First Printing, 2020

ISBN 9798649440493

www.meligoodell.com

More from Lanie Goodell

3

Salvagium (horror/romance)
Lunae Lumen (paranormal mystery/romance)
Daddy Loves Me (children's picture book)

Numerous shorts can be found at
www.meligoodell.com

For the little girl who loved the Brothers Grimm, who grew up to love everything dark and twisted about them even more than she used to.

Part One

Once upon a time, as snowflakes fell from a bitter cold sky covering the ground in a chilly blanket that shown in the moonlight, a beautiful Queen sat wrapped in fur on the window seat of her castle bedchamber. The Queen focused on the needlework in front of her, glancing occasionally at the flakes falling rapidly outside the ebony frame of the window. In one such moment, as her gaze was drawn to the window, she missed the fabric with her needle, stabbing the alabaster skin beneath. She gasped, drawing her hand from beneath the fabric. As she watched the blood collect on the tip of her finger, the tiny drops oozed down her hand to fall gracefully to the snow covering her window sill.

Mesmerized by the striking contrast of her deep red blood on the pristine snow, the Queen began to imagine the child she was carrying, the child that would soon be here, saying aloud to the empty room: "Would that my daughter grow into a beautiful woman, with hair as black as this window frame, skin as white as the snow beneath my hand, and lips as red

as the drops of blood that fall from my finger to grace
the snow beneath my hand."

When her daughter was born, the Queen was pleased
to see her porcelain skin was flawless. Her ebony hair
flowed in tight curls, framing her cherubic face. Her
daughter's cherry lips turned up in childish laughter
daily, the brightness of her smile enchanting those
around her. The Queen named her Snow White.

The Queen was the most beautiful woman in all the
land. Her beauty was her most prized possession and
the quality she admired most in herself and her
daughter. She became enraged, filled with anger and a
jealous passion, whenever she felt as though a woman
may be more attractive than she. Upon her marriage to
the King, she had been gifted a magic mirror by a local
witch. Each morning, she stood before the mirror,
contemplating the beauty bestowed upon her.

"Mirror, mirror on the wall, who is the fairest of them
all?" the Queen's musical voice would call through the
empty bed chamber, the daily question falling from her
lips as easily as if they were part of her soul. While the
witch had been careful in her directions that the Queen
ask only specific questions and that she understand
answers would be only those directly related to the
question asked, the Queen had never needed to request
anything of the mirror but for the question she asked it

that morning. Indeed, she had never requested a single bit of information from the mirror but the solitary question.

The Queen knew the response, as it told her each morning that she was, indeed, the fairest of them all. The Queen craved this validation of her beauty; the sheer acknowledgement that she was the most beautiful woman to exist.

As Snow White grew, she became more beautiful with each passing year. The Queen was enamored by her daughter's beauty, the obsession of a possession instead of the love of a parent, but that soon began to fray as Snow's beauty began to surpass that of her mother. Upon waking one morning, the Queen was ensconced by a sense of dread. As she combed her long auburn curls, she once again asked the magic mirror her question, the words no longer flowing from her mouth like music but dripping from her lips as though they were a curse she was bestowing upon herself.

"Mirror, mirror on the wall, who is the fairest of them all?" her voice trembled as she spoke.

"My Queen, though you are beautiful, tis true, Snow White is much more beautiful than you."

The Queen grew cold with rage. Her rage grew into hatred of the girl to whom she had given life, for she knew the mirror could not lie and that Snow White had taken her place. From that moment forth, each time she gazed upon her daughter, the hatred burned deeper within her until it was all consuming, overtaking her soul. The Queen's obsession became unrelenting, tormenting her to the point where her daily ablutions no longer held any form of relaxation.

Days turned into years as the mirror repeated its damning phrase each morning. The words began to echo in her thoughts throughout her waking hours. Before long, the damning phrasing haunted her dreams, driving her deeper into the madness that encompassed her soul. As the words continued to follow her, the Queen could focus on little else than her hatred for her daughter. She tossed and turned in her bed each night, replaying her daughter's childhood. Each playful moment of her life, which could have been so easily snuffed out in those formative years; each missed opportunity to rid herself of the child's presence. From the moment they were spoken, the words followed the Queen, until one day she knew what she must do. The Queen called for her most skilled huntsman.

The man stood before her in the throne room. She admired his strength. His long, golden locks were tied tightly at the base of his neck. The leather vest he wore over the flowing fabric of his tan tunic was battle scarred, betraying his past and the apparent skill of his hunting. As she admired his appearance, the Huntsman silently appraised the Queen's ragged exterior. The once lustrous locks fell in a dull mess around her shoulders. The alabaster skin drew taught across now too sharp cheekbones. The once beautiful queen was nothing but a shadow of her former magnificence. The Huntsman knew better than to show his surprise at her appearance or the drastic change that had taken place since he had last stood before her. For all her beauty, his Queen was known to also be vindictive and any negative reaction on his part would mean certain death. While his life was nothing grand, he did not want to lose it.

"I cannot stand to look upon my daughter once more. You are to take Snow White to the forest. You must choose a secluded area, far from the village. It is here that you will slaughter her. Ensure that she suffers, as I have suffered since she stole everything that I am. As proof of your success, you will bring me her heart. I will cook and eat the fresh muscle to restore myself to my former glory."

The huntsman once again hid his shock and vowed to obey his queen. He knew that to do otherwise would mean an end to his own life, though this task would bring him none of the joy that hunting usually brought. He was skilled, that was true, but his love of the hunt always resulted in fresh meat to bestow upon the village. This task was nothing more than an assassination brought about by the jealousy of a mad queen. There was no honor in the deed, nor would there be joy in the delivery of Snow White's heart.

That very night, the Huntsman led Snow White away from the castle. Though she was confused at his sudden appearance, as well as the request that she join him on his hunt, her eyes sparkled with excitement at the prospect of adventure, for she spent many hours locked away in the castle, wishing to see more of the country surrounding her stone prison.

They walked through the village. The Huntsman reminded her several times that the villagers were sleeping and it would be rude to awaken them. Days started early in the village and Snow White's excited utterances were sure to be noticed. *The villagers would surely come to the princesses aid if they were to find her alone in the dark with me,* the Huntsman thought as they made their way between the humble cottages that speckled the town.

They walked quickly into the woods surrounding the small community. Night grew darker as the trees enveloped the light from the moon, casting eerie shadows on the ground beneath their feet. Snow White gasped at the creatures of the woods scurried away from their approaching footsteps. She moved closer to the Huntsman with each howled cry that cut through the near silence of the forest, seemingly taking comfort in his presence. They walked for many hours until the woods were almost too dark to see and the area was deserted.

Snow White pushed through the brush and into a clearing. Moonlight glistened through the canopy of trees, still blocking the majority of light. She smiled as she turned circles in the clearing, raising her arms out beside her and laughing into the silence that surrounded them. Completely free and comfortable with herself, the Huntsman found himself entranced, watching her with rapt attention for too long. Shaking himself free of her beauty, the Huntsman pulled his knife, preparing himself to carry out his orders. His heart raced as he crept toward the glowing princess. Each muscle trembled in anticipation of the dreaded task which had been forced upon him.

Snow White turned, calmly looking him in the eye. A stream of moonlight broke free from the canopy of leaves and glistened off the blade of the knife. She took two steps forward, slowly lifting her hand to place it along the Huntsman's cheek. He shivered at the chill of her flesh along his fevered skin. The task with which he had been given frayed his nerves, sending a fever through his body. His arm slowly sank to his side, the knife falling from his weakened grasp to land with a gentle thud on the dirt floor of the woods. Snow White tilted her head slightly. Her brilliant blue eyes stared into his.

"You do not wish me harm, dear Huntsman. My mother has insisted you do an unspeakable act in the name of envy. You are noble and her orders are beyond that which you are capable of doing. You will return to my mother, alerting her of my demise. In return, I shall run, far from here and I shall never come back to the village nor step foot into the castle again," her voice trickled through the woods around them, lulling the beating of his heart. Snow White stroked the Huntsman's cheek; the back of her hand grazing the pounding vein of his throat. The Huntsman was bewitched by the music of her voice, unable to move away from her or tear his eyes from hers as she gazed through him and into his soul. Every particle of his being wished to please her.

After several moments of silence, the Huntsman nodded. He slowly bent to retrieve the knife and sheathed the blade in his holster as Snow White stepped away from him. His heart skipped a beat, noticing how stunning she looked beneath the light of the moon. Her pale skin shown in the milky white light; white as death beneath a veil of infinite darkness.

"The beasts, m'lady?" his voice shook as he forced the words from his mouth. He desired to protect her from the darkness surrounding them, while he knew the beasts would do the job for which he'd set out to accomplish. The thought of her delicate flesh being torn by the vicious teeth of the animals shook him more than the Queen's rage when she discovered he had failed to execute her will. As did the image that flashed through his mind of his own teeth upon her skin.

"They will not harm me," Snow White smiled. "But they will come for you as soon as I have left this clearing. I trust that you will sever the heart of one such beast and present it to my mother as proof of my death. I would not want her to take her vengeance out on you, Huntsman. It is not you that she wishes dead."

A small tickle at the back of his thoughts gave the Huntsman a momentary pause. Snow White knew much of the plans her mother had enforced upon him. He briefly wondered why she had come to the woods with him so willingly. Gratitude at her compliance washed over him.

Snow White blended into the night. The Huntsman heard the footsteps as she fled the area, moving quickly through the darkness, never faltering. Sorrow washed through him as he accepted that he would never see her smile grace the moonlit night again, his heart now thoroughly captivated by her essence. As she had promised, a young, wild boar entered the clearing following her departure. The Huntsman quickly cut its throat before setting to the task of removing its heart. He expertly severed the still beating organ from its host with stealth and efficiency.

The Huntsman returned to the castle. He knelt before the Queen, presenting the heart of the boar as proof that Snow White was no longer alive. The Queen laughed in anticipation of her meal, sending the heart to her cook immediately to be prepared with salt and onions. Her laughter echoed through the castle as she ate her meal, glorying in the knowledge that she was, once again, the most beautiful woman alive.

Part Two

Snow White ran through the woods, lightly leaping over fallen tree trunks and skipping over holes in the soil. She glided over the forest ground as if floating a mere inch above the surface. She listened carefully to the sounds of the forest, taking note of the wild animals that seemed to avoid her path. A small smile graced her lips as she considered being the most dangerous predator in these woods. Her dress caught on a thorn as she ran by a prickly bush, tearing the sapphire silk. She hardly noticed as she drifted through the woods. She ran for miles, covering her shoes and clothes in mud and moss. At one point, the heel of her slipper caught the jutting branch of a fallen tree, snapping the shoe in half. She sat, gracefully pulling the slippers from her feet and discarding the ruined material before reclaiming her previous speed, the soil against her skin cool in the night. She never tired, growing stronger with each graceful leap across the dirt beneath her. The morning glow was beginning to glint across the horizon, setting the mountains in the distance on fire with the warmth of the sun. Snow White caught a glimpse of a light far from her..

Increasing her speed, she ran toward the pinprick of lamplight.

A tiny cottage sat in a clearing just outside the forest. The light she had seen was cast from the lamp beside the door, to lead the inhabitants to the right location. She walked slowly toward the cottage, aware that there were no sounds from within. She watched the meadow surrounding the cottage as she moved, attentive to any attack, but sure she'd outrun any threat the Queen could have sent her way had she believed the Huntsman would fail.

Snow White knocked loudly on the heavy oak of the cottage door before trying the handle. The knob refused to budge, though she insisted. The sun was higher in the sky and Snow White felt tired, too drained to continue forth, feeling increasingly heavy as the sun grew brighter. She looked around the clearing. A small woodshed sat beside the main home, the door standing open. She looked inside, finding a large pile of wood and just enough room for her to curl up on the floor beside it. She closed the doors as the sun broke over the mountains, signaling the start of a new day.

She slept beside the wood throughout the daylight hours and did not wake until she heard the sound of men singing. Glancing around the wood shed, she blinked rapidly, trying to remember where she was.

The previous night's events rushed through her mind, jarring her into sudden consciousness. Her skin prickled with tension as she listened to the men singing. Footsteps on the earth beneath their feet thundered through her ears. She rose slowly, brushing the now dry mud from the silk of her dress and righting the fabric. Though torn and dirty, the gown was still obviously a sign of her noble status. Snow White cracked the door of the shed and peeked through. Six tiny men skipped toward the house, lunch pails swinging as they walked. A seventh man brought up the rear, practically stomping as he growled at his brothers. She squared her shoulders, smiling sweetly as she left the shed and walked toward the men, making her appearance as harmless and innocent as she could.

"Good evening," she said, her musical voice carrying through the quiet, night air. The men stopped, swiveling around to look at her in astonishment. She smiled, demurely folding her hands at her waist as they examined her appearance. The tear in her dress was quite large and noticeable, as were the tangles in her waist length curls. Though she had wiped the mud from her dress, the stains remained and her slipperless feet were all muddy and showed wear from the forest rocks over which she had run.

"Oh, goodness," one of the men exclaimed.

"Who are you?" the stomping man asked, his grumpy tone affecting Snow White not at all.

"My name is Snow White," she answered sweetly. "My mother, the Queen, ordered a huntsman to kill me. He graciously spared my life, but I have been running all night. When I stumbled upon your little cottage, I knocked, but no one was home. I slept in your wood shed for I was too tired to walk any further." Snow White let her hands fall to her sides, her shoulders slumping in a sign of defeat.

The tiny men, dwarves to be sure, though Snow White had never before met a dwarf, looked between themselves. They nodded, as if coming to an unspoken agreement.

"Surely you are hungry," said one.

"And thirsty," piped another.

"You must want to get clean," offered another.

"Humph," grunted the surly dwarf who had demanded to know who she was.

Snow White nodded, once again smiling sweetly at the men. The irritable dwarf narrowed his eyes, as if sensing there was more to her story. Snow White met his eyes, silently compelling him to believe her. She stared intently into his brown orbs, never letting her icy blue gaze falter. After a long moment, the angry little man huffed again before nodding at the others.

"If you will keep our house," the cantankerous man muttered, his gruff voice hesitant but unable to suppress the offer. "By this we mean you must handle the cooking and sewing, the washing, and making the beds, as well as keeping the house tidy. If you do these things, and do them well, you may stay for as long as you need. Our house is well off the traveled path and our work keeps us too busy to entertain. There will be no one here who can reveal your location to the Queen. You will be safe in our home." The offer was grudgingly given, but sincere nonetheless.

Though not accustomed to the work they described, Snow White readily agreed to their terms, aware that the Queen would only be satisfied with the beast's heart until she awoke and spoke to her mirror. The cottage was smaller than her bed chamber in the castle and she was sure she could figure out how to complete the chores that would grant her asylum. Snow White glided toward them, grateful for a place to sleep off the ground and a place to hide from her mother. They walked toward the door, each dwarf speaking quickly, asking questions over each other that Snow White had not the chance to answer before the next was asked.

Snow stayed silent, letting them drag her along with them, though she had no interest in their garbled excitement. The dwarves crowded at the door, pushing each other in their enthusiasm. Snow White deftly escaped the shuffle, pausing on the small front step. She watched as they threw their work gear on a bench just inside the door. She glanced around the somewhat cramped space of the cottage. The room was small, but tidy and welcoming. Seven small beds lined the back wall. Each was made with crisp corners, the bedspreads pulled tightly across the mattresses. A long dining table took up most of the kitchen, benches along both sides to accommodate the many men. The kitchen sink was stacked with dishes, though the pile was neat and organized, allowing for quick cleaning once the men returned home from their work. A sitting area was arranged between the beds and the kitchen. Three couches had been pushed together around a large coffee table that was scattered with books and mugs of half-drunk coffee.

The dwarves looked back at her expectantly, their voices falling silent as they waited for her to enter their home. She looked at them, her visible discomfort causing looks of confusion to grace the happy faces. The angry dwarf huffed at her once again.

"Well?" he grunted. "Aren't you going to come in?"

Snow White smiled, her discomfort melting from her rigid shoulders. She nodded before taking her first step into the tiny home. The air around her smelled of cinnamon and dirt from the mines. Her nose wrinkled, the smell of sweat became more prominent as the men removed their mining jackets.

"Of course," she said softly, responding to the cranky man as an afterthought. "Thank you for your warm welcome. I'm sure this will be a pleasant experience for us all."

She gently closed the door, placing her hand on the oak slab and quelling the burn in her throat. She took a deep breath before turning back to the little men.

As the men slept, Snow White carefully cleaned their home. Moving silently around the space so she did not disturb the men in their tiny beds, she wiped each surface until it shone. The rooster began to crow as she finished setting breakfast on the table. Snow White grunted at the sound, realizing that this was to be a completely different experience than the one in which she had grown. The rooster had obviously been trained, or enchanted, as the sun was hours from cresting the mountains. The men awoke to find seven steaming bowls of porridge surrounding the now glistening table. Each place was set with sparkling silverware, steaming cups of tea, and crisp snow white linens. The men leapt from their beds, drawn by the intoxicating scent of their breakfast. They stumbled over each other to thank Snow White for her work.

"You did not sleep, Miss?" asked one of the dwarves as he shoveled porridge into his mouth, immediately yelping at the heat of the fresh meal. Laughter filled the table as he blushed at his mistake. Snow White chuckled as she handed him a glass of cold water.

"I slept all day yesterday. I was not tired," she said softly, taking a seat on the nearby couch as they enjoyed their meal. Snow White kept her tone gentle each time she spoke to the men, giving them the illusion that she needed more protection than she did.

"You will be tired today. You may use my bed if you wish," offered another, his blue sleep cap slipping over his eyes in his excitement to please her.

"Or mine!" exclaimed another, his mouth full of freshly baked bread. The other dwarves nodded in agreement, each offering his bed to the young woman of which they suddenly felt very protective. All but the grumpy man.

Snow White watched the man, his face screwed up in a scowl as he sniffed the porridge. He carefully took a bite before deciding it was edible and taking another. He set his spoon down, buttering his bread while he swallowed the porridge. He never looked at Snow White, nor did he speak as he silently ate the breakfast before him. Snow White smiled at the other men as they praised their food, each asking for seconds while they told her about their jobs in the mines. Being small men, they were able to fit into small spaces, making them an invaluable part of the mining team. While they spoke, Snow White nodded, murmuring her responses, demurely sitting on the edge of the couch. Her mind, however, was engaged in thoughts of the angry little dwarf and whether he was to be a problem in her desire to avoid death. He obviously did not trust her, something she rarely encountered. She nodded politely as the men spoke, appearing to engage in the conversation with the six other men, however she used the time to think through ways to gain the seventh's trust.

"We work early."

"We leave before dawn."

"Do not expect to see us before dusk, Miss."

"There is food in the cupboard and more in the root cellar."

"I hope dinner is as good as breakfast!"

"We haven't eaten like this in years!"

Their comments pleased Snow White. She had never cooked a meal before and was not at all sure she would know what to do. It had taken her two tries before the porridge was not cement and inedible. She had always been a quick study and was pleased with her success.

Snow White cleared the table as the men readied themselves for the mines. She removed the lunches she had prepared while fixing breakfast from the icebox and packed each pail before handing it to one of the seven men as he left. The surly man was last, stomping across the room to grab his pail. Snow White gently laid her hand on his arm as he reached for his pail.

"I hope my being here does not inconvenience you," she said as she stared into his eyes. He stared back, the chocolate brown orbs bore into hers. His movements stilled as he gazed at her, seemingly entranced by her watchful stare. He shook his head. Snow White smiled. "I am glad. I do not wish to be a burden."

Snow White released his arm. The man shook his head as if clearing the cobwebs that surrounded his thoughts. He stumbled toward the door. He glanced back at her and started to huff before changing his mind. Confusion grazed his usually grumpy expression. She smiled at him, encouraging him to continue on his way.

"During the day you are to be alone here at the house. Though we are not on a well traveled path, you are a hunted woman. It will not be long before the Queen realizes her plan has failed and she will send additional people to complete her mission. It is best you do not open the door for anyone." He shook his head once more, the protective speech puzzling him. He rarely felt protective of anyone, especially a woman he was not at all sure he liked. With that, he closed the door.

Snow White sighed. Her energy was waning. Though the sun had not yet appeared, it had been far too long since she had fed and his words worried her a bit. He was right. She knew her escape was a temporary solution to a more permanent problem. She was, more or less, a sitting duck; especially in her weakened state.

As she tidied the kitchen, washing and drying the dishes and wiping the counters until they shone, Snow White contemplated how long she would be able to stay in the small cottage. The Queen was mad, but her intelligence was unmatched and Surly was correct with his assessment that it would not be long until the Queen discovered her assassination attempt had failed. It would take only as long as the time in which the words traveled from her lips to the mirror. Though the men would be nothing more than collateral damage if the Queen were to discover her hiding place, she would prefer not to have their blood on her hands.

Senseless killing had never been her style and she would prefer to keep it that way.

When the kitchen was once again glistening, and the sun finally graced the meadow with its gentle morning beams, Snow White lay across one of the beds. Her frame was taller than the mattress, but the soft material felt wonderful against her tired back. Within moments, she slept, her dreams haunting her.

The princess turned fitfully in the bed.

Part Three

Many miles away, the Queen was sleeping peacefully for the first time in years. She had eaten every morsel of her daughter's heart. The rage and hatred that had consumed her for so many years seeped away with each bite, leaving the Queen in a restful place, ready for the next step in her recovery.

The sun pouring through her open windows woke the haggard queen. She stretched, feeling the sweet relief that came with releasing her anger. She smiled to the empty room. The Queen took her time dressing, brushing her long hair until it recovered some of the luster that had once graced the locks. She drifted around her room, humming softly as she twirled, letting her skirts fly out around her. She stopped in front of the magic mirror, once her most prized possession, though she could not yet bring herself to look at her appearance in the glass.

"Mirror, Mirror, on the wall, now who is the fairest of us all?" she sang beautifully, awaiting the response that would bring her fully back to her old self.

"My Queen, while you are the fairest in this land, Snow White, across the woods, is the fairest since time began."

The Queen froze. Her hands went numb as the blood seeped away from her heart. She felt light-headed and stumbled for a nearby chair. She screamed in pain as the betrayal of her most trusted huntsman washed over her. Realization that the seven dwarves, the only inhabitants of the area beyond the woods, were hiding Snow White gave the Queen a starting point for rectifying the mistake the Huntsman had made.

The Queen stared at the mirror, looking into the glass for the first time, hatred of the object and of her daughter returning. Her skin had not regained any of its brilliance and the luster of her curls was just an imagined effect of her mood as they hung limply across her shoulders. She sat for a long time, pondering her next move for she would know no peace until the mirror proclaimed her the fairest once more. Hours passed as the Queen revised the plot in her mind, reworking angles until she was sure it would work. A slow, evil smile spread across her face, settling in her eyes as they turned to onyx in the now fading light of day.

The Queen called her Huntsman to her, sure he would do her bidding now that she knew the fear in which he must live. Handing him a list of supplies, she sent him to gather them, allowing him only an hour to do so. She took pleasure in the tell-tale quiver of his hand upon her list.

While he was gone, she collected the things she would need from within the castle. Upon his return, she closeted herself in her room, dying her skin an ugly shade that marked years of time in the sun. She ratted the long curls, streaking them with oil from the kitchen to give herself an unwashed appearance. Taking the clothes the Huntsman had gathered, she dressed carefully, ensuring they hung on her frame so as not to betray her figure, the only portion of her youth she had retained. Finally, she padded the back of her right shoulder, hunching forward to further conceal her shape. She smiled at the old woman in the mirror. Not even her own parents would have recognized her had they not been dead many long years.

Taking a horse from the stable, careful not to attract the attention of the guards, she rode toward the woods. The trip was long, even on horseback, and it was just before dawn the following morning when the Queen arrived at the clearing in which the seven dwarves lived. She watched as the little men hummed as they walked the path to the mines. Once they were out of sight, the Queen dismounted. She hobbled toward the cabin and rapped on the door. Snow White answered quickly, no doubt assuming one of the dwarves had returned.

"Pretty things, my dear? I am the old peddler, here with bargains to offer such a lovely young woman," the Queen rasped out, concealing the voice she was sure Snow would recognize as her mother's.

"What have you got to sell?" Snow White asked, staring at the basket the queen carried. Her tone was not that of the grateful young child the Queen had raised, but that of a savvy buyer.

"Laces, dear child," the Queen's razor blade voice crooned. "Such beautiful silk laces as you've never seen. Would you care to see?" When Snow White nodded, the Queen pulled a yellow, red, and blue silk ribbon from the basket and held it out to her daughter.

"How pretty!" Snow exclaimed, stroking the ribbon.

"Would you care to buy?" The Queen was sure of the response. Her daughter had always enjoyed pretty things and this ribbon was in the exact shades of Snow White's favorite colors.

"Yes," Snow White said eagerly, nodding at the old peddler. *Surely, this old woman can do me no harm,* she thought. She'd stayed inside, the door in her hand for protection, ready to slam it in the face of any oncoming attack. She beckoned the old woman to follow her into the small cabin, reaching into the bag she'd brought from the woods that contained the only money she had carried with her from the castle.

"Oh dear!" the Queen exclaimed upon assessing Snow White's gown. "How did you dress so carelessly this morning, my child. Surely you must have someone to help you with those laces. Come here and I shall change the laces and do them up properly for you."

Snow White smiled, knowing the gown was rumpled and dirty from her run through the woods and that the laces were the least of her worries. She'd had only the dress in which she'd escaped and the seven little men had no fabric with which she could craft a new gown. She nodded to the old woman, pleased with her seemingly oblivious concern for the state of her ties. Snow White turned her back to allow the Queen to replace the laces of her blue gown. The Queen replaced the laces quickly, tightening them to the point where Snow White could not breathe. The girl gasped for breath, her face turning an unappealing shade of red then darkening to purple as she struggled to reach the ties at the back of her dress. As her daughter passed out on the floor, the Queen laughed gleefully and hurried from the cabin.

"I am, once again, the fairest!" she shouted to the trees as she rode swiftly through the woods.

In the cabin, Snow White gasped, taking one long breath before sitting up and undoing the laces of her dress. She glared at the door of the cabin, left open as the Queen made her escape. She rose slowly, wondering if the Queen truly believed her dead this time. Snow walked purposefully toward her bag, taking a small flask from its depths and sipping at the room warm liquid, feeling it's life force fill her veins. She carefully corked the flask before stowing it once again in the depths of the bag. Wiping the dark red substance from her lip, slowly licking it from her finger, she glared at the retreating hoof prints she could still hear echoing through the wood.

The Queen had made one grave mistake in her attempt to murder her daughter. Snow White was already dead.

****

When the seven little men returned from the mines that evening, Snow White told them of the visit from the Queen disguised as the old peddler. The Dwarves were terrified as Snow White described what had transpired, though she assured them the Queen had not hurt her, having left the ties looser than she must have thought. In reality, Snow White was lucky she did not need breath to survive. The Queen had pulled the laces tightly enough to leave cuts along her back.

The Dwarves chattered over each other, making Snow White promise not to again open the door to anyone while they were at work in the mines. Surly stood behind the others, arms crossed, as he watched Snow White tell her story. He seemed to be dissecting her words as she spoke and Snow White knew she would need to speak with him alone again, to push his conscious mind to suppress his unconscious suspicions.

***

When the Queen returned to her castle, she immediately called for her bath to be drawn. She scrubbed her skin until the pink glow returned, washing all the dye and oil from her skin and hair. She took her time with her toilette once she stepped from the cooling water. Humming to herself as she combed her hair into a shining mass once more, she stepped toward the mirror.

"Mirror, mirror, on the wall, *now* tell me what I must hear. Who is the fairest, far and near?" The Queen smiled broadly as she stared at her glowing skin in the mirror.

"While you are a beauty, it is true. Snow White, beyond the wood, is more beautiful than you."

The Queen froze. The blood drained from her face as she realized that she had failed once again. She screamed, throwing her hair brush toward the mirror. It bounced off the frame, falling to the floor with a crack. Footsteps echoed through the hallway outside her door as servants ran to protect their queen.

"STAY OUT!" she screeched at the staff as the pounding of fists against the heavy door echoed through her bedchamber. She stormed across the room and threw herself across the bed. The Queen spent the rest of the day and long into the night meditating on her options. The task of disposing of her daughter was proving more difficult than the Queen had expected. The Huntsman was known for his heart of stone and yet, Snow was able to convince him to spare her life. The seven dwarves were known to avoid society, never allowing anyone into their home or onto their land; but Snow White was able to weasel her way into their home and under their protection. The laces were tied tightly, Snow's skin blossoming into the rosy glow of asphyxiation and she still lived. The Queen ran through her options, the gravity of her next choice weighing heavily upon her as she delved deeper into the darkness of her decision.

Poison! she thought. The Queen sat abruptly in bed, glancing at the moon high in the black of night. *Potent poison that she'll not escape from easily.* There was a mushroom that grew at the edge of the woods known to all as certain death. The Queen, having grown to maturity in this area, knew how to harvest the mushrooms without doing harm to herself. She decided to soak them in garlic oil, to leach the poison from the mushroom itself while she rode. The Queen pushed herself from the comfort of her bed and hurried across the room to her dressing table. Rifling through the objects, she found the elaborately elegant comb for which she was searching. A small, evil smile crossed her face as she stroked the golden comb, a gift from her father before she had pierced his heart with a dagger.

Disguising herself differently than for her first trip, the Queen gathered the supplies she would need before slipping through the darkened castle and into the woods. The horse's hoofs thumped the moist Earth as she rode quickly through the trees. She pushed her horse to run faster than before; the galloping hooves beating in time to the pounding of her heart. Even without her disguise, it was likely no one would have recognized this crazed woman as their queen. Her eyes blazed with a fire lit by the Devil himself.

It was midday as the Queen tied her horse to a tree at the edge of the woods. She had not slept in more than a day and the bags that hung below her eyes were proof that she was beyond exhaustion. Still, there would be no sleep until her mission was complete. Until she was finally rid of the seed of her jealousy and hatred. She crossed the open area, limping slowly to conceal her stride. Knocking on the door to the cottage, she pasted a kind smile upon her face as the curtain fluttered to reveal Snow White's curious look.

"I cannot let you in, Ma'am," Snow White said clearly through the window.

"But surely you can look?" the Queen replied, her Gypsy accent thick. She had wrapped her head in beautiful scarves, kholing her eyes to replicate the exotic look of the Gypsies that would travel through their kingdom. The Queen pulled the comb from her basket, carefully avoiding the tines she had dipped in the poisoned garlic oil.

Snow White's gaze fell upon the comb. She recognized it as her mother's most prized possession and the last gift her grandfather had bestowed upon his daughter before someone had killed him. *Mother must be desperate to be rid of me if she is willing to part with the comb,* Snow White thought. *Perhaps I can reason with her and let her know I have no wish to return.* She opened the door, welcoming her mother into the cabin once again.

"This comb will look beautiful in your raven hair," the Queen exclaimed in her fake accent, unaware that her daughter saw through the disguise. "Come, come child. Let me place it so you might see how lovely you will look."

The Queen ushered Snow White over to a chair at the table. She ran her fingers through the black strands, arranging them carefully before lifting the comb. Snow White watched her mother in the reflection of a nearby mirror. She hardly recognized the gleam of hatred that now graced her mother's one magnificent eyes. She felt nothing but pity staring at the woman in the mirror. Once full of life, the drawn skin was dull and lacking in health. It was obvious the Queen had not slept well recently and she wondered if her mother had even attempted to sleep since her last visit. Snow watched her mother raise the comb several inches above her head. With all her strength, the Queen jabbed the comb into Snow White's hair, seating the tines deeply into her skull.

Pain radiated through Snow White's head as she collapsed beside the chair. She gasped for breath, confusion and panic radiating through her mind.

"Hmmmmm," the Queen murmured as she watched her daughter writhe on the floor at her feet. "That should have killed you instantly. No matter, you shall be dead before your seven petite protectors return from their mine. By then, I will be long gone and no one will know I was here."

The Queen wiped her hands on the folds of the skirts she wore, a nervous gesture as she'd, moments before, been holding a poison more deadly than all others. Without another glance at her daughter, she strode from the cabin and into the sunlight. She was sure that, this time, she had not failed.

Inside the cabin, Snow White lay gasping for breath. It was breath she did not need, but was automatic in light of the pain that cascaded through her person. She struggled to lift her hand to the comb embedded in her skull. The movement pulled at the hair trapped beneath her. Snow cried out in pain. Her fingers dragged across the rough wood of the floor, trailing through the pool of blood forming under her head. Her brow knit in confusion once again at the sheer amount of sticky

liquid that seemed to seep from her body. Her thoughts
flashed, drawing her back in time as she lay dying.

*The man in front of her was not more than
twenty from his looks. Long, auburn hair gently
fluttered in the spring breeze. He smiled,
beckoning to her from across the meadow
beside the castle.*

*"Princess, you are alone?" he asked, his voice
like melting honey on a hot summer day. Snow
White nodded, wondering if she should fear this
man. She'd slipped away from her governess, a
dowdy old woman who found no joy in
anything, so she might frolic in the meadow
and gather wildflowers.*

*"Fear me not, Princess," the man murmured as
he approached. "I am not here to harm you.
Indeed, I am here for the same reason as you.
To enjoy this magnificent day."*

*Snow White had fallen in love with him that
day. She had met him everyday forth, for weeks,
until her governess finally discovered her route
of escape and put an end to her days in the
meadow. It was then that Snow White realized
how miserable life in the castle made her. She
sent word to the man, the son of a local
merchant, to meet her at the edge of the woods*

*the next morning. She packed a satchel,
prepared to escape the castle permanently. Her
sixteen year old heart could not be bound by
the castle walls any longer.*

*He was there, as she had requested, the next
morning. A smile played across his beautiful
full lips as she snuck around the village to meet
him. Wrapping her arms around him, she
reveled in the strength of his embrace.*

*"Take me from here," she said into his chest.
"Let us run away and never return."*

*"But Princess, your life is here. I cannot be the
reason you abandon your kingdom," he said,
burying his face in her hair. She smelled of
milk and honey, a fresh promise of tomorrow.*

*"I cannot stay here a moment longer," she
pleaded. "Surely I will die amid the stifling
watch of my governess."*

"What if..." his voice trailed off.

*"What, my love? Please, tell me." Her small,
porcelain hands gripped the rough fabric of his
tunic.*

"What if I could give you the ability to stay, with the knowledge that they cannot turn you into something you do not wish to be?"

Snow White nodded, begging him for the secret. He kissed her then; their first kiss in the bright sunlight of the last day of her natural life. Snow felt her heart explode with the intensity of her love for this man who she'd known such a short time. Her skin burned beneath the chill of his lips as he trailed his mouth along her neck.

"Do not be afraid, my love. I will never, never leave you," he whispered against her feverish skin.

The pain was sudden and intense, but soon turned to pleasure as his teeth tore into the skin beneath her ear. She gasped, pushing closer to him as every nerve, every vein, was set flaming by the sensation. The world began to spin. Her eyes flew open. The world, so very bright, began to dim. She grew limp in his arms. He lowered her to the ground, removing his mouth from her throat. As the world blackened, her last vision was of his mouth curving up to smile at her, two fangs gleaming in the sun.

She awoke many hours later, ravenous and craving something she could not put into words. Her love, the man that she had begged to take her away from this place, sat beside her on the ground. His eyes were focused on something in the distance, but he smiled as she stared at him.

"You have awakened," he murmured. Her ears, much more sensitive now, reveled in the smooth tones of his voice. She lifted a hand to stroke his hair away from his face, finding her arm to be as light as a feather.

"What... what has happened?" she asked.

"You are... different now, love. You are as I am. Both human, and yet, more. Do not be afraid. I am here. I will teach you." And he did.

They spent every moment possible together. It was months of happiness that Snow White never imagined possible. That is, until he was no longer there.

Snow White struggled against the slow death oozing through her veins. She had thought herself immortal until this moment; immortality proving to be a promise much like that of the love she had shared with a man who had disappeared from her life. The stupidity of her death bombarded her consciousness. She had known her mother was there to do her harm, but her arrogance

had prevented her from acting. Now, she lay dying.
She thought of Alaric and the promise of eternal
strength. The strength now leaving her as the world
once again blackened. She would never find him now,
never know why he broke his promise to never leave.

That night, the seven dwarves returned home as they
always did. Trudging up the path to their home, they
found the cabin dark.

"Where is Snow White?" they muttered to each other,
varying levels of concern evident in their voices. As
they approached the cabin, the silence began to gnaw
at them and they rushed inside. Finding Snow White
lying in a pool of blood, they sprang into action. It took
four of them to lift her and carry her to the nearest bed.
The pillow beneath her head stained red immediately.
One of the little men examined her head while another
ran for a clean cloth and another for fresh well water.
Finding the comb, they pulled it free, carefully
avoiding the tines as the stench of the garlic oil alerted
them to the poison. As soon as the comb was removed,
Snow White's eyes fluttered open. The wound began
to ooze more slowly.

When the water arrived, the surliest of the men
snatched the cloth from his brother, dipping it quickly
in the bowl and washing the wound. He glared at Snow
White.

"We told you not to open the door to anyone," he snapped, dipping the cloth again into the now crimson water. Snow White was too weak to object and, not knowing how to defend herself, decided it was not worth the effort.

Once her wound was cleaned, the little men went outside again to wash before fixing dinner, as Snow White had lain dying instead of meeting her daily chores. The angry man stayed behind, still glaring at his unwelcome house guest.

"You know the Queen will not stop before you are dead. All the way dead. She will return, Princess, and she will not leave until the deed is complete," he crossed his arms. Though small in stature, Surly made up for his diminutive size in presence. His attitude angered Snow White, for she was perfectly capable of protecting herself now that she understood her limitations. She took a slow breath to contemplate her response. She knew this man was the weak link in her ability to stay in the cabin. Her previous attempts at compulsion, a skill that accompanied her immortality, had proven ineffective long term.

"Yes, I know. I was not aware of the lengths to which my mother would go to dispose of me," she whispered, a pitiful expression of insecurity carefully playing across her sad expression. Surly relaxed a bit, lowering his arms and staring at her.

"You must promise not to open the door. For anyone this time, Princess. We barely made it in time to save your life. Next time, you may not be so lucky."

"You are right. I promise," she murmured, masterfully playing the role of victim.

The man's shoulders slumped as he sank to sit on the bed beside her. His brows still drew together in a show of displeasure. Snow White held out her hand, silently asking him to take it. He did, reluctantly holding her cold hand in his.

Snow White brought it to her face, kissing his knuckles. Surly shifted uncomfortably, obviously uneasy with the show of affection. Snow White turned his hand over and sank her teeth into the flesh of his wrist, hungrily gulping the fresh blood from his wrist. She was too weak to recover on what she had left in her flask. She drank, feeling the strength weakening in his arm. It was hard, so hard, to make herself stop, but she needed him alive. He stared at her, groggily blinking his eyes. She met his eyes, her stare intense.

"You will not remember this," she said firmly. He nodded. "You will allow me to stay. You will be pleasant toward me for you do not suspect me of

anything. You will believe what I tell you." He nodded
again and Snow White suspected that her compulsion
would work this time. She had been too weak from
lack of blood and he had been too strong. The tables
had turned.

She raked a nail along her own wrist, feeding him a
few drops of her own blood to return his strength
before ordering him to join his brothers at the wash bin
outside. As he left the room, Snow White lay back
against the pillow. Her nose turned up in distaste at the
stench of the poisonous blood that coated the fabric of
the pillow. Pulling it from beneath her head, she leaned
back against the second pillow, sinking into the plush
feathers. The men would expect her to be weak from
her blood loss and the trauma of the afternoon. She
would use this time to find a way to defeat her mother.

***

The Queen returned to the castle, storming up the stairs
to her bed chamber. Without taking off her Gypsy
disguise, she ran to the mirror on the wall, anxious to
hear the words she missed so deeply.

"Mirror, mirror on the wall, tell me this moment, who is fairest of them all," she demanded, her manic screech making the glass tremble.

"While you, my Queen, are fair tis true, Snow White remains much lovelier than you."

The Queen howled, tearing pieces of her costume off and throwing them around the room.

"How?!" she hollered to the empty space. "How does she live?"

The glass on the mirror rippled, as an image of Snow White appeared on the surface of the glass. The Queen stood frozen in place, rage trembling through her veins, as she watched her daughter bite into the dirty flesh of the dwarf beside her. Comprehension washed over the Queen as a slow ice began to form in her stomach.

"She is fairer, I see, through the work of the Devil," she whispered. The Queen then remembered the man locked in her dungeon, the pale, beautiful man with whom her daughter had tried to escape her destiny. She changed quickly, donning her most regal gown and piling her hair on top of her head before placing her crown upon the top of her hair. She marched down the stairs, new resolve making her steps more confident. She descended into the dungeon. The guards stood at attention as she passed, sending each other a look of apprehension as the Queen had never come to them, favoring to meet with their prisoners in the great hall. She swept by the men, giving them no more than a cursory glance, before ordering the keeper of the keys to take her to Alaric.

The man huddled in the corner of his prison room. Emaciated and grey, he did not lift his head as she approached. The keeper of the keys banged the metal bars with his keys to get Alaric's attention.

"Kneel in the presence of your Queen, crooked-nose knave. Have you no respect?"

Alaric lifted his head slowly. He painfully got to his knees, looking the Queen directly in the eye. His impertinence amused her now that she knew the playing field. As the keeper of the keys rushed to open the door to discipline him for his disrespect, the Queen saw the flash of hunger in Alaric's eyes and stopped the key keeper before he could open the door. She did not need Alaric at full strength. Dismissing the key keeper, she kept her eyes trained on the man within the cell.

"I believe I was mistaken in my original assessment of your sins," she stated calmly. The man before her cocked his head slightly, amusement filling his hungry eyes.

"It appears that your crime was not assisting the princess in her foolish attempt to abandon her right to the throne. Am I right in assuming that you are the one who has, in fact, killed my daughter?"

"Your Highness, it seems as though you have already decided that to be fact," he replied.

"Yes. It is, indeed, a fact. The problem, you see, is not that she is dead, for I have attempted to make that more permanent. The problem lies in the fact that you have made her immortal." At this statement, Alaric's eyes widened. His jaw twitched as though he were going to speak, but he thought better of it.

"You are surprised by this, since the crime for which I have you locked in this dungeon was assisting my daughter in trying to leave. There was a time when I would do anything to keep her here with me. That time has passed," the Queen paused for breath. She measured her next words carefully before continuing. "No creature is truly immortal. There is a way to dispose of her and you shall tell me how."

Alaric's eyes narrowed as he glared at the Queen.

"Why do you believe I would share that information, Your Highness?"

"I will give you your freedom once the task is complete. If you chose not to tell me, your days here will be long and hungry. I am sure you have been feeding on the rats that enter your cell as the bread the guards provide would give you no sustenance. I can assure you, no living thing will enter your cell should you choose not to provide me with the information I need."

Alaric's stoney expression filled the Queen with satisfaction. She had not felt so in control since Snow White had been deemed more lovely than she. She waited, watching the man weigh his life against that of her daughter. She was pleased when he glanced at the corner as a rat scurried across the floor and out of sight. His shoulders slumped as he sank further to the floor.

"You'll need to pierce her heart with a wooden stake. It is the only way to kill us. She is weaker during the daylight hours. If you attempt to attack her once the sun has set, you will surely die in her place," Alaric's voice was full of self hatred as he shared this information with the Queen.

She carefully controlled her expression, ensuring he could not see the glee that filled her. Without responding, she turned and walked quickly from the dungeon. She rushed up the stairs.

The Queen knew Snow White was unlikely to allow her into the cabin once more. She would need a rouse much better than her previous ones. She entered the secret room behind the mirror, so secret that she was the only person who knew of its existence. She prepared a poison apple, knowing the poison would not affect her daughter, but would give the fruit an appeal that would be hard for anyone, even a cursed immortal soul, to resist. The Queen set off once more for the dwarf's cabin, knowing this would be her last trip through the woods.

The Queen slept on the mossy earth just within the wooded area beside the cabin. As the sun reached its peak in the sky, the warmth of the beams against her skin woke the sleeping woman. Smiling at her good fortune, she quickly crossed the meadow and rapped once again on the door.

The Queen heard footsteps as Snow White stopped on the other side of the door.

"I'm sorry, but I cannot open the door for anyone," Snow called from inside.

"I have simply come to offer you apples from my orchard. I live nearby and often deliver ripe, juicy apples to the seven men who live here." There was a pause before Snow White opened the door.

"Would you like an apple?" the Queen asked Snow White.

"Thank you, but no. The dwarves would not be pleased if I took anything."

"Do you fear poison?" the Queen asked, smiling kindly at her daughter. "Here, I shall cut this apple in half. I will eat one side and you may have the other."

Snow White watched the woman, who she had not yet recognized, bite into her juicy half of the apple. It was surprising to discover how much she wanted the other half, having not craved any real food since becoming immortal. She gratefully took her half of the apple, biting into the succulent fruit. She groaned in pleasure, the juice running down her throat as smoothly as fresh, warm blood. So engaged in eating the fruit was she, that she did not see the Queen remove a wooden dagger from the basket she held. Without giving Snow White a chance to prevent the attack, the Queen seated the dagger in her chest. Snow White fell to the floor of the cabin, the last piece of her apple rolling across the floor.

The Queen kicked at Snow White with her shoe, taking no chances that she was truly dead. When her doubt was satisfied, she ran across the woods. Hopping on her horse, she rode swiftly through the forest.

Once back at the castle, she skipped up the stairs. Rushing to the mirror, she practically sang the words she'd repeated so often recently:

"Mirror, mirror, on the wall, who is the fairest of us all?"

"My Queen, though Snow has recently been, tis you that is fairest, once again."

The Queen started to laugh. She laughed so hard she could no longer stand and sank to the castle floor. The laughter continued until her sides hurt and tears streamed down her face. She crawled to the bed, exhausted.

"Now I shall have peace," she murmured as she fell into a deep sleep.

Part Four

The men came home that night to find the door of the cottage standing open. They rushed as one to the entrance to their home to findSnow White lying, pale and lifeless, on the floor just inside the door. They checked the laces of her dress, finding them tied loosely. They checked her hair for signs of another poisoned comb, but again came away with no explanation for what had killed her. They shook her, yelling her name repeatedly in an attempt to revive her. It was almost an hour before the men gave up. Surly seemed consumed by the task of waking her, much to the surprise of his brothers.

When they finally resigned themselves to her death, they carried her gently to the couch. Laying her body along the velvet covering, the men sat and wept for their companion. Surly, tears flowing freely from his swollen eyes, sobbed into the skirt of Snow White's gown, cursing the Queen and all who knelt at her feet.

The men stayed in mourning for three days. At some point, two of the men left, returning with a glass casket in which they laid the body. Even in death, Snow

White looked magically alive. Her pale skin seemed to glow and her lips still held a shade of red so similar to the apple they'd found beside her that they could not bear to place her in a wooden coffin. Surly engraved her name into a golden plaque placed on the side of the glass. He purposefully left her ancestry off, though it was customary, in protest of the evil actions of the Queen.

The men took turns staying home. Each day, while his brother's worked the mines, one of the dwarves kept watch over Snow White's body. As time passed, the season's changed, and the sky marked the passing of the years, Snow White's body remained the same. The men continued to mourn her loss, though Grumpy sank further into his grief with each passing day.

Many years after the fateful day the men found Snow White dead, a young man approached the cabin. His long, flowing hair and palewhite skin reminding the men of their lost princess.

"Please, might I rest in your home?" the young man asked. The seven dwarves, having just returned from the mines, were filthy. They eyed him cautiously, taking in his expensive clothing and the cleanliness of his hands. They had no way of knowing that the clothes were taken off the man's last meal, or that the hands had been recently cleansed of their bloody state in a stream by the dwarves' home.

"Who are you?" Surly grunted. He'd lost all trust in people the day his princess had died and could not believe this man was here without evil in his heart.

"I am Alaric. Please, I am not here to do you harm. I was a prisoner of the Queen for many years, unjustly accused of an act I did not commit. I am recently released and on my way to my own land. I seek only rest in your home." Alaric felt this story would give them peace, and hopefully entrance to their home. His land was the same as theirs, but they had no need of this knowledge or of his true identity.

The seven dwarves glanced between each other. Surly, eyes narrowed, acquiesced to the wishes of his brothers, allowing the man to enter his home though he was still suspicious.

"Please, sir, give no mind to my brother, for he is still in mourning. You are welcome in our home," the shyest of the men said, warmly welcoming Alaric into the cottage. Alaric smiled back at the little man and stepped into the small home. It was then that he saw the coffin. He stared at it quizzically.

"That is Snow White. She was the daughter of the Queen," the shy man offered, watching Alaric gaze at the coffin.

"How did she die?" Alaric's voice was rough as he asked.

"We are not sure. We came home one day and found her. We have kept her in this glass box since then. The years have passed, but she does not change. She appears as though she were but sleeping, however, no breath does she take."

Alaric ran his fingertips over the glass above Snow White's lips. It was then that he saw the small tear in her gown, directly above her heart. He remembered the conversation with the Queen. The glint of evil in her eyes had betrayed her plans, though Alaric had been sure that Snow White would overcome the weak human body of her mother. When word of the Queen's success had reached his ears, Alaric was overcome with grief, and unconcerned with the broken promise of his release. He had only escaped now, upon news of his father's passing, in order to see to the affairs of his family before killing himself.

His mind rolled through his possible actions as the men prepared dinner. He sat quietly as they ate, memorizing the drawers out of which they pulled various cooking utensils. As he settled into the couch that night, he let his exquisite hearing take control, listening to the breathing of each man as it became slow and measured, indicating they were all asleep.

Alaric crept silently from the couch. He pulled the cover of the coffin free, running a finger along the icy skin of the woman he loved with his whole being. Fumbling through the layers of fabric, he felt the wooden stake in her chest. Alaric used the corkscrew he'd taken from the kitchen to get a firm hold of the wood. He pulled, hard, dragging the wood from her chest in one stroke. She gasped, her eyes flying open.

Snow White sat abruptly. As Alaric carefully watched, the wound began to heal. Snow White blinked rapidly, trying to get her bearings. She grabbed the edges of the coffin, raising herself out of the glass to step lightly on the ground beside her. She looked around, seeing Alaric for the first time.

"You are… you are alive!" she whispered in amazement.

"As are you, my love," he whispered back. Alaric took her face between his hands and kissed her. It was the kiss of lovers who had walked through fire and back just to be with each other.

Snow White's eyes grew red with hunger. Years without feeding had taken their toll on her self-control and she shoved Alaric out of her way. She moved swiftly, the confident movements of a predator stalking her prey. Her eyes found the angry dwarf through the darkness of the cabin. She sat on the bed beside him, watching the pulsing of his blood through his carotid artery. Covering his mouth with her hand to muffle and shrieks of terror, she let her teeth tear at the artery, greedily drinking the warm, rich blood that she so desperately needed. He struggled, but she was too powerful for him to get more than an inch in any direction. She felt the life flow from his limbs as she drank each drop. He soon stopped writhing. Moments later, he stopped breathing. The blood flow became sluggish as she drained his now lifeless body.

She hungrily tore into the next man. Alaric watched in fascination as the woman he loved became the monster he had created. His throat burned with need and he followed suit. They fed, often together, on each of the men in turn. As the sun began to creep above the mountains, they surveyed the room. Blood painted the walls an eerie red that sparkled in the morning light. The bed sheets were soaked through. Alaric and Snow White were also covered, but they did not care. Snow White drew a dagger from its sheath at the waist of one of the men, slipping it into the pocket of her dress before turning to Alaric. .

They made love in the pre-morning mist, surrounded by the evidence of their crimes of the night before. Donning their ruined clothing, they set off to find the Queen, and make sure she got exactly what was her due.

Part Five

Snow White took her time on the trip back to the castle. There was much she had missed in the years since the Queen had staked her, sending her into a state of perpetual suspension. Though Alaric had been in a suspension of his own, slowly starving in self punishment for the hated act of telling the Queen his beloved's vulnerabilities, he told her of the news that had trickled into his prison cell.

"It was not the worst thing to have happened," Snow White said, gently stroking her hand along his icy cheek as they cleaned themselves of the Dwarfs' blood in the stream running through the forest. She could see how much his betrayal had cost him and her heart, though no longer beating, still broke for him.

"It was not what you deserved," Alaric responded, his voice filled with years of regrets. "I assure you that my admission came only after I decided there was no way the Queen could best you. Your strength is far superior."

"Had she not been my mother, there is no way she would have beaten me," Snow White admitted. "I am grateful her aim was not truer, for I would not have been able to survive had she known the precise location of my heart."

The sounds of woodland creatures cut through the night as they continued along their path. As morning began to overtake the forest, Snow White led Alaric to a cave near the edge of town.

"I played here as a child," she explained, leading him deep inside the cool rock. "We will be safe here until night falls once more."

"As time passes, the sunlight will not affect you so. Though my time in the Queen's dungeon was not pleasant, it did strengthen me and the sunlight no longer has the same effect." Alaric's voice was strong and true, his eyes searching his true love's face as he spoke. The years he'd spent in the dungeon, thinking her dead, had aged him. Though there would be no outward sign, his heart showed the strain.

Alaric curled into the corner of the rock room, lifting his hand to Snow White. She arranged her skirts around them. The lover's slept, wrapped in each other's cold embrace, throughout the daylight.

They woke at twilight, the eerie glow of the dying light casting long shadows into the cave.

"It is time," Snow White murmured, her eyes bright with the excitement of vengeance.

The castle lay on the far side of the village, it's magnificent turrets illuminated by the light of the moon. Armed guards stood at the entrance, though their attention was not focused on incoming threats.

"It has been many years since there was a threat to the castle or the Queen. Tales of her sorcery, her ageless beauty, reached far and wide. Neighboring kingdoms fear her wrath," Alaric explained through the dark. They were perched behind a boulder with clear sight of the castle entrance.

"Will not the guards notice that I have not aged?" Snow White asked as Alaric led her toward the entrance.

"They will think it but another act of sorcery from your mother," he assured her.

"Halt!" yelled one of the men. "Who goes there?"

"It is I, your Princess. Kneel before me," Snow White commanded, entering the light from one of the torches.

The guard's eyes grew wide. He fell to his knees, his head falling forward as a sign of respect.

"We thought you dead, m'lady," he said.

"As does my mother, I am sure," she responded assessing the situation. The death of the guard would be easily accomplished, though her spry mind was not sure his death was to her best advantage. She moved closer, her brilliant blue eyes focusing on his.

"You shall tell no one of my return," she said, her voice taking on the ethereal tone she'd used on both the grumpy dwarf and the Huntsman so many years ago, entrancing the guard with its otherworldliness.

He nodded and rose as she beckoned him to do. She and Alaric slipped through the gate, their heads bowed so they could avoid further recognition. Though there were still a few people skittering through the courtyard, they were pacing themselves far enough apart that it was easy to keep their distance. Snow White slunk beside the wall surrounding the courtyard, her eyes locked on the door to the castle.

They slipped through the door unnoticed by the rest of
the court, the night growing older and the people
growing tired. Snow White marveled at the familiarity
of the castle, though it had been many years since she
had last laid her slippered foot on the staircase rising to
the bedchambers. Then, laughter had filled her lungs
with air, a joyous expression crossing her beautiful
face. She had always been pleased, content to walk the
halls of the castle, knowing that, when royal life
became too much, her meadow would offer her retreat.
Now, as she slunk through the darkened halls, her feet
bare of their former regal attire, she made no noise.

***

The Queen had grown comfortable as the years had
passed. She knew of what the neighboring kingdoms
spoke. She knew of the magic she supposedly
possessed and it gave her a sense of peace. Following
the death of her daughter, the Queen had not aged, as
was the promise of the mirror. Her power lay in the
dark, mystical forces of death and no one, whether they
be from her kingdom or another, was willing to test the
extent of that power.

On this night, the night of her death, the Queen was
still blissfully unaware of the threat to her person. She

combed her luxurious hair, once dull, until it shone
almost as brightly as the mirror. She scrubbed her face
until it was pink and dressed in her favorite sleeping
gown, the same shade of sapphire blue that her
daughter had worn the day the Queen had killed her.
She no longer felt regret for the loss of her daughter,
knowing the demon she had become before the Queen
had rescued her. As the years passed, the details
became muted, and she became a heroine.

She climbed beneath the cool satin sheets of her bed,
content that another day was done and she was still the
most magnificent creature in all the lands. The mirror
had assured her of this fact the morning before. The
Queen, so sure that no other would grow to maturity to
take her place, no longer felt the need to check the
mirror on a daily basis. She had no doubt that there
would never be another as beautiful as she.

Soft noises from the hall made the Queen sit up. The
moon seen through the window of her bedchamber
confirmed that it was quite late. Shuffling feet gave her
pause before she discounted the sense of danger that
emanated throughout the chamber. Deciding herself
foolish, and the sounds mere footsteps from the guards,
she sank once again against the soft pillows that
adorned the head of her four poster bed. She closed her

eyes against the night, dreaming peacefully of her gown selection for the following day.

A hand, cold and icy, slipped over her mouth. The Queen's eyes flew open, her breath catching against the vice of the chilled fingers. She fought to see the face of her attacker, but the shadows of night swallowed the figure, leaving only the inky outline of a person. She struggled to breathe, the air growing thick in her lungs, before her vision dimmed. She sank into the grateful escape of unconsciousness as laughter tickled through the bedchamber.

***

Snow White fastened a set of iron shoes to her mother's feet, wondering at the brilliance of Alaric's plan. While in the dungeon, he'd experienced all forms of torture her mother could devise. Upon discovering his true nature, she was interested in pushing his immortality and exploring how much he could endure. As such, Alaric was well aware of what devices were at their disposal.

The Queen's eyes fluttered but stayed closed as the shoes were locked in place. Snow White attached their chain to the matching iron that hung from the ceiling of the torture chamber. She pulled, reveling in the feeling of power as her mother was slowly raised, her hair swinging inches above the stone floor of the dirty room.

"Shall we wake her?" Alaric asked, his eyes drawn to the expression of his beloved's face. Her exploration of the room had amused him, though he would have preferred not to be in the space. Her interest was almost obsessive as they planned her revenge. In the end, the Queen had used her power to take everything from Snow White, and so now, they would remove the beauty she so desperately craved.

"Let her wake on her own. Look, her eyes now flutter. It will not be long."

Snow White took her place in front of her mother, crouching so her face would be the first image the Queen saw. She smiled as her mother's eyes opened, growing fully wide as the horror of her situation took hold.

"Hello, Mother," she said, her musical voice bouncing off the walls and echoing before disappearing into the night.

"Snow White?" the Queen asked, her voice weak.

"You thought you had rid yourself of my life. That was not the case."

The Queen's eyes flickered to Alaric, fear replacing her confusion. Alaric raised a hand to his chest, his bow a mocking gesture of her stature.

"You're going to kill me," the Queen acknowledged.

"We will, indeed," Snow White answered.

Alaric moved back, propping himself against the wall of the chamber and allowing Snow White to honor her need to vengeance against her mother. While his claim would have been just as valid, he felt as though this was something his love would need if they were to be truly content in their life together.

Snow White, her eyes shining, cut the long curls until her mother had but only patches of hair covering her scalp. She drew the dagger she had stolen from one of the dwarves from the bodice of her gown, drawing stars along her mother's cheeks before shredding the nightgown she wore so the pretty fabric hung in strips about her person.

"I am truly regretful that your need to be the fairest of us all led you to death, Mother. It is a tragedy to be sure," Snow White murmured as she sank her teeth into her mother's milky white throat.

The Queen, her screams unheard by anyone but Snow White and Alaric, grew silent as Snow White drank from her. Alaric followed suit at the motion of his love, sinking his teeth into the opposite side of the Queen's neck.

When the Queen was dead, her glassy eyes staring at nothing and her body drained of all it's blood, Alaric released the iron shoes, catching the corpse before it hit the ground. They carried her back to her chamber, laying the no longer beautiful woman in bed. Snow White opened her wardrobe, pulling a golden gown from inside and changed out of the ratty dress she'd now worn for too many years.

She stepped in front of the mirror her mother had cherished more than her own daughter.

"Mirror, mirror, on the wall, who is the fairest of us all," she asked, smiling into the night.

"You, Princess, are fair and true, the most beautiful maiden around is you."

Snow White glanced at the pitiful body of her mother, her heart surging with justice.

"Magic mirror, hear my plea, no longer shall you answer questions for you are free."

The mirror shimmered, the magic sparkling as it seeped out of the mirror and soaked into the floor of the bedchamber. No longer would the mirror grant answers. No longer would the magic create obsession. No longer could anyone be controlled by their desires.

Taking Alaric's hand in her own, Snow White led them from the castle and into the stables. As they rode through the countryside, her laughter rang over the hills and through the empty meadows. Snow White, like the magic of the mirror, was finally free.

The End

About the Author

Lanie Goodell grew up in Asheville, North Carolina before travelling the United States with her parents and her son in a pop-up camper. They started in the mountains of North Carolina, trailing through the center of the country, and up the Pacific Coast, before winding up in Denver, Colorado. She writes about the places she's been, feeling grateful that she has first hand knowledge of so much of the United States.

Holding degrees in both criminal justice technology and psychology, Lanie loves to weave both disciplines into her stories, making them both realistic and entertaining.

When she's not writing, Lanie is either hanging with her teenage son or substitute teaching in the Denver area. She has recently discovered a passion for teaching theater and will be doing that through the rest of the 2019-2020 school year. She is also a sometimes long-term substitute at a charter school designed for immigrants. It's been a wonderful experience that has allowed her to learn about cultures from around the world from the people who have lived in them.

For more about Lanie and her exploits, visit www.meligoodell.com or follow her on Twitter at www.twitter.com/lanig321.

www.ingramcontent.com/pod-product-compliance
Lightning Source LLC
Chambersburg PA
CBHW021340160726
47994CB00007B/2782